TOUCHED
BY AN
ANGEL

Fear Not!
A STORY OF HOPE

Written by MONICA HALL
Illustrated by KEVIN BURKE
Based on a Teleplay by KEN LAZEBNIK

MARTHA WILLIAMSON
Executive Producer

Based on the television series created by JOHN MASIUS

Tommy
NELSON

Thomas Nelson, Inc
Nashville

Published in Nashville, Tennessee, by Tommy Nelson™, a division of Thomas Nelson, Inc. Executive Editor: Laura Minchew; Managing Editor: Beverly Phillips.

Library of Congress Cataloging-in-Publication Data

Hall, Monica
    Fear Not : [a story of hope] / written by Monica Hall ; illustrated by Kevin Burke ; based on a teleplay by Ken LaZebnik ; produced by Martha Williamson.
       p.   cm. — (Touched by an angel)
    "Based on a teleplay by Ken LaZebnik."
    Summary: At Christmastime, visiting angels bring hope and strength to Joey, a boy who is terribly afraid of the dark, and Serena, an African-American girl whose critical heart condition does not give her long to live.
    ISBN: 0-8499-5800-8
    1. Angels—Fiction. [1. Courage—Fiction. 2. Fear—Fiction. 3. Guardian angels—Fiction. 4. Christmas—Fiction. 5. Afro-Americans—Fiction. 6. Christian life—Fiction.] I. Burke, Kevin, 1969– ill. II. Title. III. Series.
PZ7.H14725Fg   1998
[Fic]—dc21

                                      98-7834
                                      CIP
                                      AC

Printed in the United States of America

98 99 00 01 02 03 WCV 9 8 7 6 5 4 3 2 1

If there's one place you might expect to meet angels, it would be in church.

But when it happened, everyone was very surprised. Everyone, that is, except Joey and Serena—a boy who was afraid of the dark and a girl whose hope and joy lit up the world of everyone around her.

But then, *they* were the reason the angels came. . . .

Every day was a celebration for Serena. But today was extra special. Serena hummed a happy little tune as she fluffed her wings and straightened her halo.

What did it matter if the choir was singing the wrong notes, the organ would barely play, and the manger was *very* shaky?

There was going to be a Christmas pageant. And *she* would be the angel!

"How do I look, Joey?"

"You look wonderful, Serena!" Joey answered.

Joey thought everything about Serena was wonderful. Just being with his friend made him feel good instead of "different."

Serena was never impatient when Joey was slow to understand things that were easy for other people. She didn't mind when he talked too loud. And she never teased him about being scared of the dark. She looked past all that . . . to the Joey inside, and just loved him.

"Oh, look at her, Tess," said Monica as they watched from the choir loft. "Isn't she a wonder! So much joy and love!"

"Yes, Baby," said Tess, "and the light that shines from within that little girl has got to brighten a lot of souls, before . . ." Tess stopped for a moment. "Before it goes out."

Just then—with a discouraged W H E E E Z E!—the organ quit.

"Drat!" shouted Edna, poking at the silent keys. "I knew this old thing would break down before I did! How can we have Christmas without an organ?"

"Hello," came the answer, "we're from the Organ Repair Service."

And there in the aisle—though no one saw them come in— stood Tess and Monica.

"We didn't call any organ service," snapped Edna. Still, they *did* need help.

In no time, Tess was rearranging shepherds and wise men, and tuning up Edna's choir!

"Okay, people," said Tess, "we'll just sing without the organ until it gets fixed."

"Well," Edna said with a snort, "it better be in shape by Sunday night!"

"This is going to be at night?" asked a nervous Joey.

"Sunday night at seven o'clock," Edna said, too busy to notice how worried Joey looked.

"Okay, Deacon," called Tess, "let's start at Serena's cue."

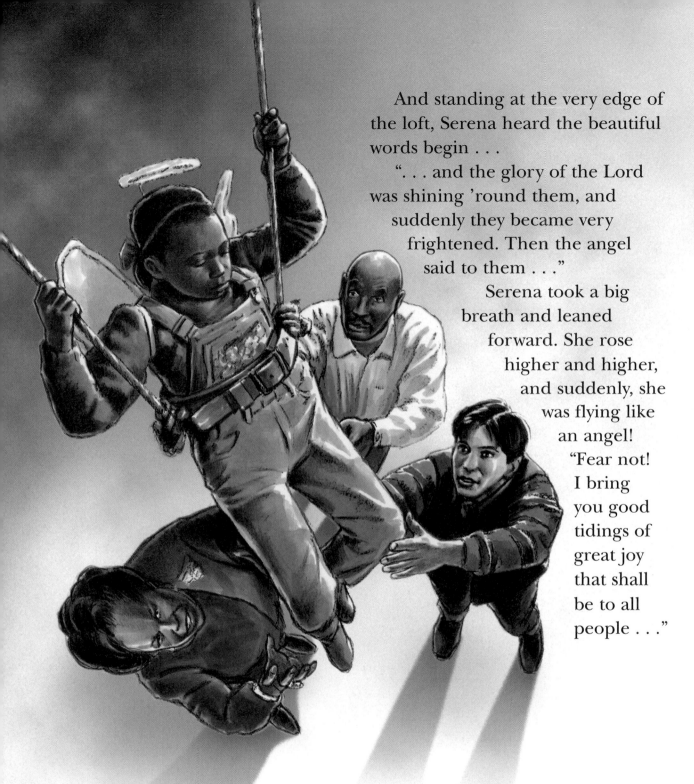

And standing at the very edge of the loft, Serena heard the beautiful words begin . . .

". . . and the glory of the Lord was shining 'round them, and suddenly they became very frightened. Then the angel said to them . . ."

Serena took a big breath and leaned forward. She rose higher and higher, and suddenly, she was flying like an angel!

"Fear not! I bring you good tidings of great joy that shall be to all people . . ."

It was wonderful! Until . . . SCREEEEECH! . . . the pulley jammed! Serena was stuck in the air. The choir gasped.

All at once, Serena's chest felt very tight. And then, she couldn't catch her breath at all!

No one saw Monica look at the rope, which suddenly began to move. It gently lowered Serena to Joey's waiting arms. "I was scared, Serena. I was really scared!" cried Joey.

"Are you all right, Honey?" asked Tess as the choir gathered around Serena.

"I . . . I can't breathe . . ." And she began to cough.

Then Monica touched her gently, and the coughing stopped. Serena sat up and said, "It's going to work, isn't it? I gotta fly!"

"You'll fly, Honey," promised Edna. "You're the only angel we've got."

"Oh, Tess," sighed Monica, "sometimes it's so hard. Knowing more than human beings and less than God."

"Don't forget, Baby," said Tess, "when God keeps you in the dark, *that's* when you start looking for stars!"

Joey and Serena were sitting on the steps outside the church.

"Are you two waiting for someone?" called Monica as she and Tess walked down the steps with Deacon Jones.

"My brother Wayne is supposed to be here," said a worried Joey. "I *have* to be home before dark!"

"He's not *afraid* of the dark," Serena said loyally. "He just doesn't like it very much."

"What if I took you two home in Tess's big red car?" asked Monica.

Wayne was upset that Joey hadn't waited at the church. "I said I'd be there. Why don't you listen?" Wayne asked.

"Monica gave us a ride, Wayne. So we could beat the dark. And Serena's here, too. We're gonna make macaroni."

"Hello," Monica said as she smiled and held out her hand to an embarrassed Wayne.

"Uh . . . hello. And thanks for bringing Joey home."

Monica asked, "Are you coming to the Christmas pageant?"

"Oh, I'm not a Christmas kind of guy," said Wayne.

"We don't have Christmas," said Joey, lowering his head.

"He means we don't make a big deal out of it," Wayne said sharply. "When our parents were alive, Mom went all out every year. But I'm too busy for that stuff now."

Monica looked into Wayne's tired eyes. She knew it was a big responsibility taking care of someone as special as Joey.

"You don't know what it's like . . ." began Wayne, leading Monica into the living room. "I'm grateful for Serena. She takes Joey off my hands for a while. Doesn't let anybody tease him or hurt him. She's probably the only one who really understands him."

"Wayne," Monica said gently, "there's something you should know about Serena."

But Wayne already knew—or thought he did. "It's her heart, right? Some kind of defect kids outgrow."

Monica shook her head. "It's a lot more serious than that. And it can't be fixed." Looking at his stunned face, she searched for the right words.

"Wayne . . . Joey is going to lose his best friend very soon."

As Monica helped Serena with her wings the next day, she smiled at Serena's favorite doll, Mr. Beans.

"Mr. Beans is going to fly with me. I promised him. An angel keeps her promise, doesn't she?" asked Serena.

Monica smiled. "Always."

Just then the choir hit a *very* sour note, and Serena said, "Why can't they sing 'Silent Night'? That's my favorite."

"We'll sing it at the Christmas program," Monica promised.

"I'm not coming to the pageant!" Joey burst out. "It's at night. And I can't go outside in the dark!"

"What is it about the dark that frightens you so, Joey?" asked Monica.

Joey was very serious as he thought about his parents who had died. "People who go out in the dark don't come back!"

Joey tried not to worry. And making snow angels with Serena
the next day made him feel much better.

When he said he was sorry for making such a fuss about the
dark yesterday, Serena understood. "It's okay, Joey. We're all
afraid of something."

"What do you do when you're scared, Serena?"

"I talk to God," she said. "Hey, Joey, why don't you talk to
God about the dark?"

"Okay," he said. "And do you think God could make Wayne
like me better, too?"

But Serena didn't answer. She couldn't seem to breathe.

"Serena!" shouted Joey. "Are you okay? Oh, my. Oh, my. Hold on, Serena. I'll get you home. Hold on." And he scooped her up in his arms and ran as fast as he could.

Joey kicked on the front door and yelled for Wayne. "Help! Help! Something's wrong with Serena!"

Wayne came running. "Put her on your bed, Joey. I'll call 911 and Serena's parents."

"Help her, Wayne. You gotta help her!" a frantic Joey called from the bedroom. Then Wayne rushed in and sent Joey outside to wait for help.

Wayne rubbed Serena's cold little hands. "Oh, come on, Serena. Don't die on me. Come on, little girl!"

But Serena didn't hear. She was looking past Wayne at something only she could see.

Right there in Joey's room—surrounded by light—were Tess and Monica. And with them, a tall man with the kindest eyes Serena had ever seen.

"This is our friend Andrew," said Tess. "He's going to take you home to heaven very soon."

Andrew took Serena's hand. His smile made her feel warm and safe. "It's going to be beautiful, Serena. And you won't feel any more pain."

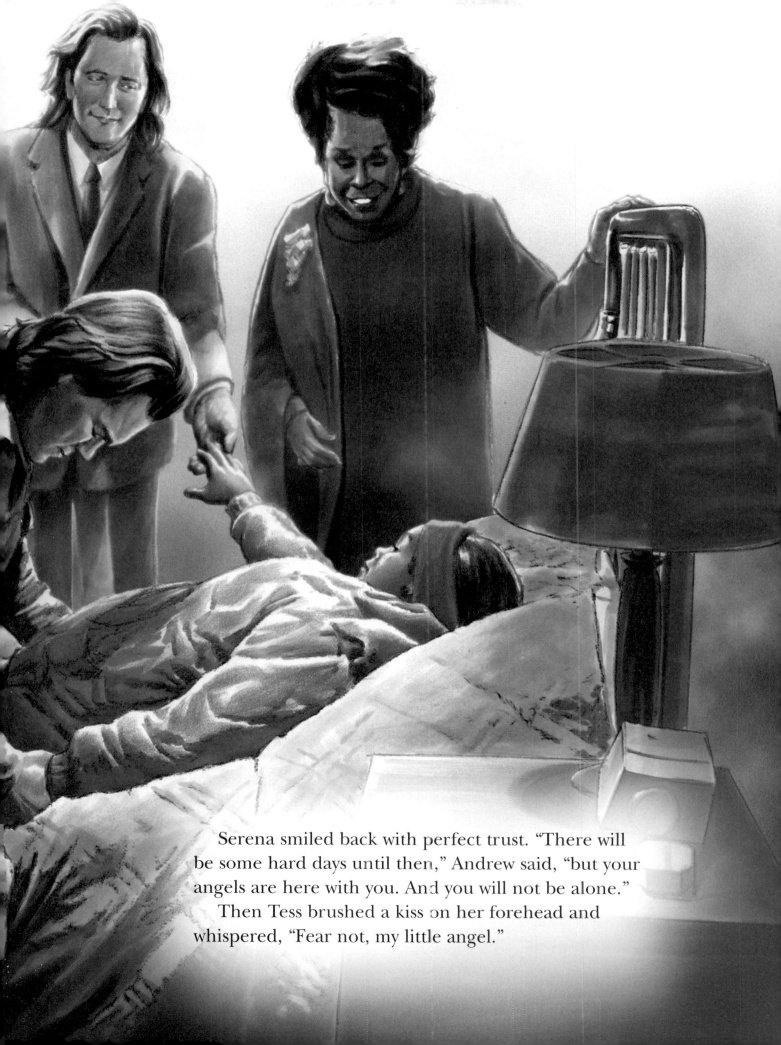

Serena smiled back with perfect trust. "There will be some hard days until then," Andrew said, "but your angels are here with you. And you will not be alone."

Then Tess brushed a kiss on her forehead and whispered, "Fear not, my little angel."

After help had arrived, Wayne tried to tell Joey about Serena. "Sit down, Joey," he said. "We gotta talk."

"Let's talk later," said Joey. But Wayne insisted. "No, Joey. We have to talk now."

Then Joey was really scared. "No, Wayne. No. The last time you said that, it was about Mom and Dad. They went out in the dark and didn't come back . . . and you said, 'Sit down, I need to talk to you.'"

And when Wayne tried again, Joey cried, "No, no, no!" He covered his ears and ran out of the house.

Out on the porch Joey closed his eyes and said, "Dear God, this is Joey. Please don't let Serena go into the dark. If she goes to heaven, who's gonna love me? Please help. Love, Joey."

He opened his eyes, then quickly closed them again and said, "Amen."

The next days were the longest in Joey's life.
But, finally, he was able to visit Serena.

And she told him something very
special. "I saw angels the other day,
Joey. Monica and Tess, the organ
ladies—they're angels."

"No!" said Joey. "Real angels?"

Serena nodded, smiling. Then she said, "Joey, you have to do something for me. You have to find Mr. Beans, and take him to the pageant. I promised him he could fly."

"But you're going to be the angel," insisted Joey. "Mr. Beans is going to fly with *you!*" Serena just shook her head.

Joey was really upset then. "I can't go to the pageant. It's at night. You have to come with me."

Serena took his hand. "I can't take you through the dark anymore, Joey. You have to do it all by yourself."

"No, no, no . . ." moaned Joey.

"You can do it." She smiled her special Serena smile. "Fear not!"

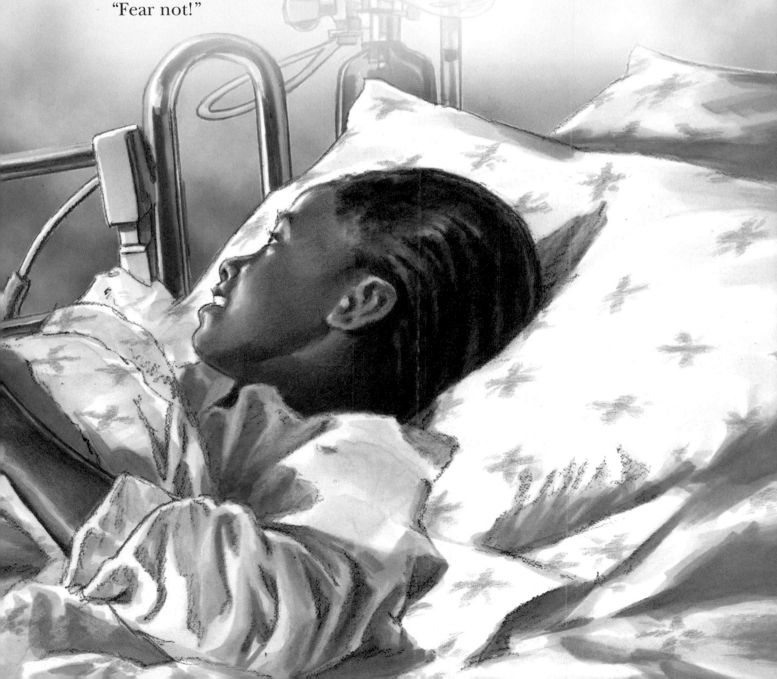

Joey wasn't sure he could do what Serena wanted. But at least he could find Mr. Beans for her!

He looked everywhere—even in church. But no Mr. Beans.

"Dear God, this is Joey again. I have a problem. I'm scared. I can't find Mr. Beans, and Serena is sick, and I promised her he'd fly, and the Christmas pageant is in the dark, and . . . and . . ."

"That's an awful lot to be afraid about all at once, Joey," said Monica.

"Are you an angel?" he asked. "Serena says you're an angel."

"Yes, I am," Monica answered.

Joey wasn't so sure. "You don't look like an angel."

"Sometimes I do," Monica said, then smiled.

"Serena is going to heaven," said Joey.

"Yes, she is," Monica agreed gently.

"I'm going to miss her. I'm going to be all alone."

"No you won't," reminded Monica. "You still have Wayne."

Joey looked at her sadly. "Wayne hates me."

Monica had to make Wayne understand! When he unlocked the lumberyard the next morning, she was waiting inside.

"How did you get in here?"

Monica just smiled. Then she grew very serious. "Do you know Joey thinks you hate him?"

"What!?" Wayne was stunned. "I do everything for him!"

"Everything," agreed Monica, "but accept him as he is! Oh, Wayne, you worry so much about the responsibility of Joey that you don't see the gift! Joey is a beautiful soul entrusted to you by God. And what he needs most from you is to know you love him . . . just the way he is."

Wayne caught his breath. Could it be that simple? "All I really have to do is . . ."

". . . love him," said Monica. "He knows he's losing Serena. And when he does, he'll lose the faith that has kept him going. He can't understand loss. But he can understand love."

It was a very sad Christmas Eve for Joey.

"I know you hurt inside," said Wayne. "I know you're worried about Serena."

"She's going to heaven," said Joey.

"We have to have hope, Joey. She's your very best friend. I think she's been a better friend to you than I have been. But, Joey, I'm going to be a better brother and friend from now on. I love you just the way you are."

Joey didn't know what to say. So, instead, he asked, "What are you doing with your suit on?"

"I'm going to the Christmas program," said Wayne.

After Wayne drove away, the doorbell rang.

"Merry Christmas, Joey," said Monica. "Are you coming to the pageant?"

"I can't," he said sadly.

"But you made a promise to Serena, didn't you?" Monica reminded him.

Joey nodded. "But I can't keep the promise because I can't find Mr. Beans."

"Sometimes keeping a promise takes a lot of courage, Joey," Monica said gently. "Serena knows you have courage."

Then she smiled and walked down the steps. And there, on the low wall around the porch, sat Mr. Beans!

Joey dashed across the porch,
grabbed Mr. Beans, and turned to
run back inside. Just then, Joey looked
up and saw something wonderful.
    A star! The brightest, most
beautiful star ever!
    And from that star, a stream
of light made a shining path . . .
right down Joey's street.

    Joey hesitated, looked at the street, looked back at the door,
then stepped off his porch into the night . . .
    And followed the star.

The pageant just wasn't the same without Serena. And the deacon's voice was sad as he began . . .

"That night, some shepherds were in the fields nearby watching their sheep. An angel of the Lord stood before them. The glory of the Lord was shining 'round them, and suddenly they became very frightened. Then the angel said to them: 'Fear—'"

Suddenly another voice joined in, ringing out from the back of the church. "Fear not! I bring you good tidings of great joy that shall be to all people! Fear not!"

And walking down the aisle—carrying Mr. Beans—came Joey! Joey, who had come through the dark to keep his promise!

Wayne hugged him. "You did real good, Joey. I'm proud
of you."

"Guess what, Wayne?" said Joey.

"What?" said Wayne, smiling at his brother.

"You love me!" Joey beamed.

And when Wayne said, "Yes, I do," Joey hugged him back and
said, "And I love you!"

And at that moment—as the choir sang with all its heart—
Monica floated out above the congregation on Serena's rope,
holding Mr. Beans.

And just as the choir reached, "Hallelujah . . . Hallelujah . . ."
Crack! The old rope snapped!

Every heart stopped. But instead of falling, Monica rose
up . . . and up!

Surrounded by bright light . . . angelic robes dancing on a
heavenly wind . . . Monica flew!

Then, with a smile for Joey, she held out Mr. Beans and
gently opened her hands. And—where Mr. Beans had been—
a pure white dove fluttered its wings and flew away.

The little church was filled with glory as a choir of angels
joined the human voices. And Herald Angels lifted golden
trumpets . . .

"Hallelujah! Hallelujah!"
And, while the congregation
watched in awe, a heavenly light
shone forth from the manger.

Then Joey saw something else. Over in the corner stood Tess and Andrew . . . and Serena!

Serena looked so happy! She smiled at Joey. He smiled back. Then he pointed up to heaven.

Serena nodded. And, with a final loving look, she waved good-bye.

At that moment, Joey knew everything was going to be okay. He knew that no matter what happened, he didn't have to be afraid anymore because God and His angels would be with him.